IN A TIZZY OVER TURKEY

by Adam Beechen   illustrated by Barry Goldberg

Ready-to-Read

Simon Spotlight/Nickelodeon

New York   London   Toronto   Sydney

Butch Hartman

Based on the TV series *The Fairly OddParents*®
created by Butch Hartman as seen on Nickelodeon®

SIMON SPOTLIGHT
An imprint of Simon & Schuster Children's Publishing Division
1230 Avenue of the Americas, New York, New York 10020

Manufactured in the United States of America

First Edition
2 4 6 8 10 9 7 5 3 1

Library of Congress Cataloging-in-Publication Data
Beechen, Adam.
In a Tizzy over Turkey! / by Adam Beechen.—1st ed.
p. cm.—(Ready-to-read)
"Based on the TV show The Fairly OddParents® created by
Butch Hartman as seen on Nickelodeon®."
Summary: Timmy revolts when his mother cooks a vegetarian dinner on
Thanksgiving Day.
ISBN 0-689-86860-X (pbk.)
[1. Thanksgiving Day—Fiction. 2. Turkeys—Fiction. 3. Wishes—Fiction
4. Fairies—Fiction.] I. Fairly OddParents (Television program) II.Title.
III. Series.
PZ7.B383 2004
[E]—dc22
2003022785

"The Thanksgiving parade was great," Timmy said, turning off the TV. "But now I am ready for a real Thanksgiving!"

"It is my favorite holiday with all my favorite foods," Timmy said, licking his lips.

"Oh, no!" Wanda cried.

"I must go pack for our

holiday trip to Mama Cosma's."

Cosmo stayed behind in case

Timmy had any last-minute wishes.

"Dinner time!" Timmy's mom called.

Poof!

Timmy sat at the table,
ready for turkey!
But his mom came in from the
kitchen carrying something
brown . . . and spongy.

"I thought we should try a vegetarian Thanksgiving this year. It is healthier," Timmy's mom said.

"So I made a tofurkey. It is turkey-flavored tofu!"

"No way," Timmy said,

stomping away to his room.

"Thanksgiving is for real turkey!

I am not eating any of that stuff!"

Timmy had a great idea.

"I know! I will wish for the best

Thanksgiving dinner ever!"

Poof!

Poof! The room filled with
junk food! There was pizza and
popcorn and cookies and candy.
"There!" Cosmo said.
"The best dinner ever!"

"I wanted the best Thanksgiving
dinner ever," Timmy said.
"None of this stuff is part of
Thanksgiving!"

"At Thanksgiving there have to be potatoes," Timmy reminded Cosmo. "And cranberry sauce and rolls! And lots of gravy! And there has to be turkey!"

Poof! Timmy couldn't believe it!

"You made beef jerky!

I asked for turkey! Lots of turkey!"

Timmy said.

"Ohhhh, turkey!" Cosmo

waved his wand again.

"Gobble, gobble" sounds filled
Timmy's room.

Timmy shook his head.

"Isn't this what you wanted?"

asked Cosmo. "Lots of turkeys?"

"Not exactly," Timmy replied.

Just then Wanda appeared.
"It looks like Cosmo did not
get your wish right," she said.
"That is for sure," said Timmy.
"One more time," Timmy
told them. "I wish I could go
to a place where Thanksgiving
is perfect."

"Okay, but are you sure you
do not want to be with your
parents?" Wanda asked.
"Hello! They're eating
tofurkey!" Timmy reminded them.

Poof! Cosmo and Wanda
showed Timmy all kinds of
Thanksgiving meals.

Poof!

Poof!

Poof!

But none was quite right.

Timmy did not think they would ever find the perfect Thanksgiving dinner. But finally, Cosmo and Wanda brought him to a quiet dining room.

The food looked perfect.

The turkey looked juicy!

"This is exactly what I wished

for," Timmy said happily.

"Well, we are off to Mama

Cosma's for dinner," Wanda said.

"I just know she won't like

my mashed potatoes."

"See you later," Timmy called.

"Happy Thanksgiving!"

Timmy turned back to the food.

He wondered, "Whose house is this?

Where are the people?"

"What are you doing here,"
someone shouted behind him.
Timmy jumped back.

Then someone stepped out of
the shadows. It was Vicky, his
least favorite babysitter.
"Tell me why you are in my
house, twerp," she growled.

Timmy thought fast. "Um, I came to wish you Happy Thanksgiving?"

"It will not be happy," Vicky moaned. "My parents and Tootie went to pick up some cranberry sauce at the store. The car broke down and they are going to miss dinner!"

"Gee, that is too bad," Timmy said,
running for the door. "See you!"
But then he caught Vicky
looking sad. That made Timmy feel a
little sorry for her.

Timmy reached for Vicky's phone.
"I know a way to make both of our
Thanksgivings better," Timmy said.
"This better not be a joke,"
Vicky warned. "Or the next time I
babysit for you . . . !"

Timmy's parents picked them
up. Next they picked up Vicky's
family, and they all drove to
Timmy's house.

Dinner was cold by the time everyone sat down to eat. "Time to carve the tofurkey!" Timmy's dad announced. But when he tried to slice it, the whole thing bounced on the floor!

Everyone laughed, even Vicky.

Tootie threw her arms around Timmy.

"I am so thankful I am sitting

next to Timmy!" she said.

"Did you have the perfect
Thanksgiving?" Wanda asked later.
"It was not what I expected,"
Timmy answered, "But I learned that
being together is most important—
even if it means tofurkey sandwiches
for lunch all next week!"